CROC O'CLOCK

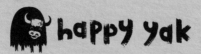 happy yak

For Kari and Nell.
HUW

For Sam, Han and Dan.
BEN

Quarto is the authority on a wide range of topics.

Quarto educates, entertains and enriches the lives of
our readers—enthusiasts and lovers of hands-on living.
www.quartoknows.com

© 2021 Quarto Publishing plc
Text © 2021 Huw Lewis Jones
Illustrations © 2021 Ben Sanders

Huw Lewis Jones has asserted his right to be identified as the author of this work.
Ben Sanders has asserted his right to be identified as the illustrator of this work.

First published in 2021 by Happy Yak, an imprint of The Quarto Group.
The Old Brewery, 6 Blundell Street, London N7 9BH, United Kingdom.
T (0)20 7700 6700 F (0)20 7700 8066
www.quartoknows.com

A catalogue record for this book is available from the British Library.

ISBN: 978-0-7112-6437-3

Manufactured in Guangdong, China CC082021
9 8 7 6 5 4 3 2 1

FSC
MIX
Paper from
responsible sources
FSC® C008047
www.fsc.org

FEEDING TIMES
1:00, 2:00, 3:00, 4:00,
5:00, 6:00, 7:00, 8:00,
9:00, 10:00, 11:00 & 12:00

CROC O'CLOCK

HUW LEWIS JONES AND BEN SANDERS

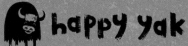

HEY, YOU. What are you looking at?

I bet you've come to see me. I'm famous…
the **BIGGEST** croc in the world!

And hour by hour I'm getting even

BIGGER!

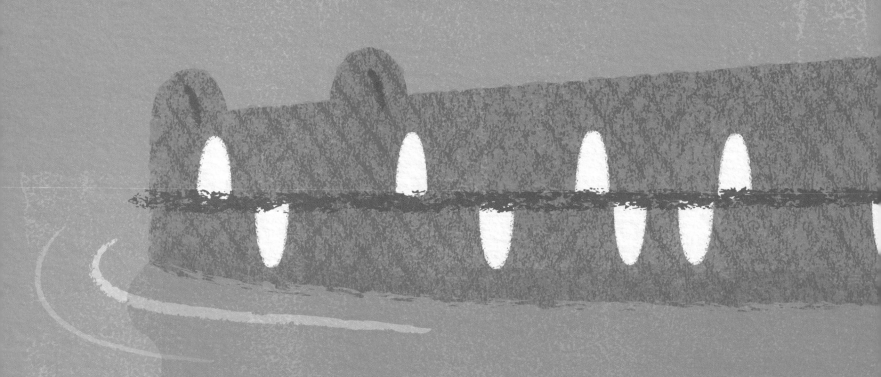

Sing with me!

At one on the zoo clock,
the keepers give to me...

A MOUNTAIN OF
MACARONI!

At two on the zoo clock,
the keepers give to me...

2 CUPS OF TEA!

And a mountain of macaroni!

At three on the zoo clock,
the keepers give to me...

3 FRENCH FRIES!

2 cups of tea

And a mountain of macaroni!

Crikey Croc, you eat a lot!

At four on the zoo clock,
the keepers give to me...

4 PUMPKIN PIES!

3 french fries

2 cups of tea

And a mountain of macaroni!

At five on the zoo clock,
the keepers give to me...

5

DOUGHNUT
RIIINGS!

4 pumpkin pies

3 french fries

2 cups of tea

And a mountain of macaroni!

*The clock ticks...
and Croc is still hungry for more!*

At six on the zoo clock,
the keepers give to me...

6 TASTY TOFFEES!

5 DOUGHNUT RIIINGS!

4 pumpkin pies

3 french fries

2 cups of tea

And a mountain of macaroni!

At seven on the zoo clock,
the keepers give to me...

7 CREAMY COFFEES!

6 tasty toffees
5 DOUGHNUT RIIINGS!
4 pumpkin pies
3 french fries
2 cups of tea

And a mountain of macaroni!

At eight on the zoo clock,
the keepers give to me...

8 MIGHTY MILKSHAKES!

7 creamy coffees

6 tasty toffees

5 DOUGHNUT RIIINGS!

4 pumpkin pies

3 french fries

2 cups of tea

And a mountain of macaroni!

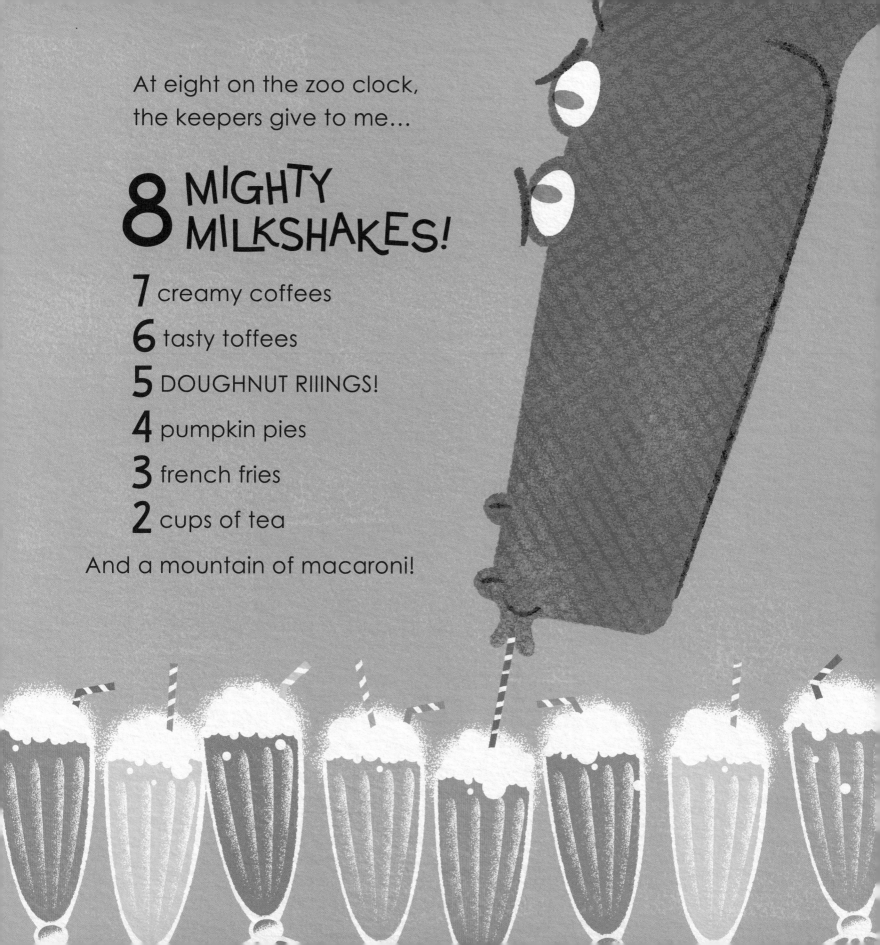

Oh Croc...
is it time to stop?

At nine on the zoo clock,
the keepers give to me...

9 CHERRY CHEESECAKES!

8 mighty milkshakes

7 creamy coffees

6 tasty toffees

5 DOUGHNUT RIIINGS!

4 pumpkin pies

3 french fries

2 cups of tea

And a mountain of macaroni!

At ten on the zoo clock,
the keepers give to me...

10 JUMBO JELLIES!

9 cherry cheesecakes

8 mighty milkshakes

7 creamy coffees

6 tasty toffees

5 DOUGHNUT RIIINGS!

4 pumpkin pies

3 french fries

2 cups of tea

And a mountain of macaroni!

At eleven on the zoo clock,
the keepers give to me...

11 LEMON LOLLIES!

10 jumbo jellies

9 cherry cheesecakes

8 mighty milkshakes

7 creamy coffees

6 tasty toffees

5 DOUGHNUT RIIINGS!

4 pumpkin pies

3 french fries

2 cups of tea

And a mountain of macaroni!

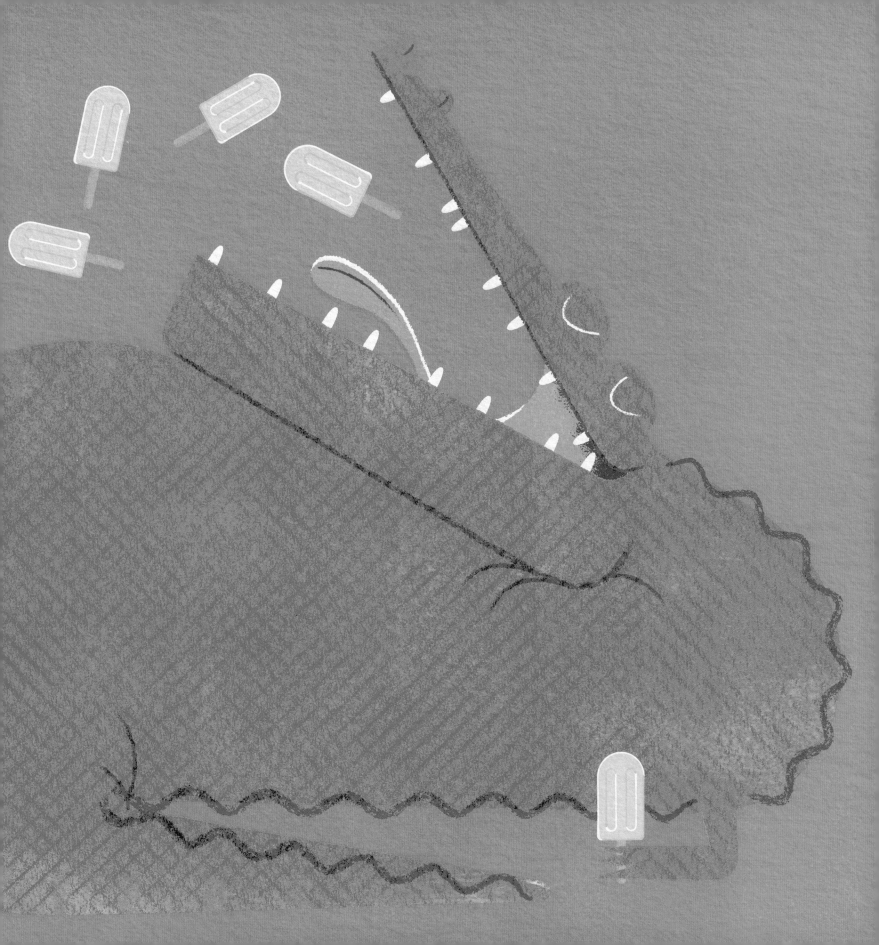

Final verse, Croc –
please don't burst!

At twelve on
the zoo clock, the
keepers give to me...

12 SYRUP SUNDAES!

11 lemon lollies

10 jumbo jellies

9 cherry cheesecakes

8 mighty milkshakes

7 creamy coffees

6 tasty toffees

5 DOUGHNUT RIIINGS!

4 pumpkin pies

3 french fries

2 cups of tea

And...

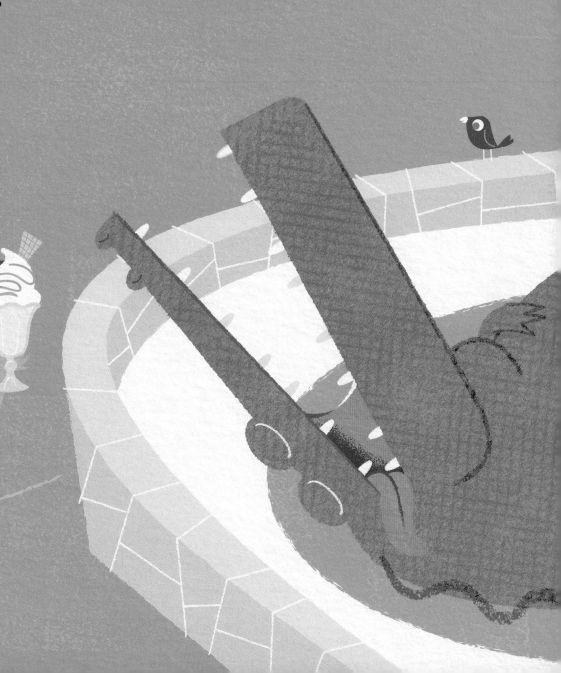

...A PERFECT LITTLE GREEN PEA!

WHAT?!

You have got to be kidding!
If I eat that **PEA** I'll surely…

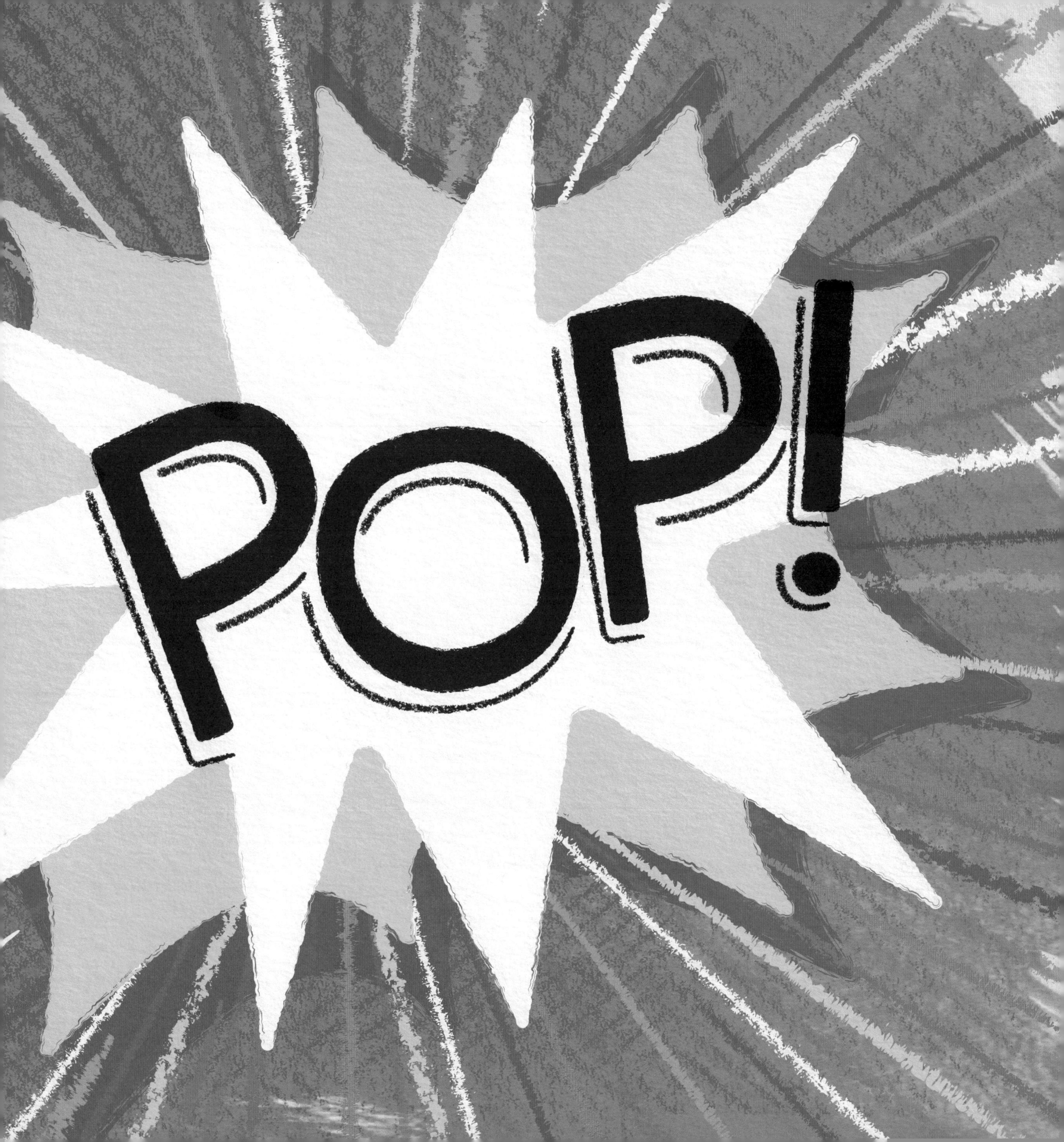
POP!

Nice try, Croc.
But from now on...

IT'S
VEGETABLE
TIME!